For my mother with all my love
from Angela Jane

For Kath, the little girl who watched with wonder
the snow from her window on Windsor Bank,
And for Clunie who has yet to discover
the magic of Christmas
S J-P

Text © 1990 Angela McAllister
Illustrations © 1990 Susie Jenkin-Pearce

First published 1990 by ABC
33 Museum Street, London WC1A 1LD

Printed and bound in Hong Kong
by Imago Services (HK) Ltd

British Library Cataloguing in Publication Data
McAllister, Angela
The Christmas Wish.
I. Title   II. Jenkin-Pearce, Susie
823'.914[J]

ISBN 1-85406-078-3

The Christmas Wish

Story by

Angela McAllister

Illustrations by

Susie Jenkin-Pearce

London

It was the night before Christmas. Everything was ready in the snow-snug town. In the market square, a giant fir tree had been decorated with wooden toys. And a fairy with a star on her wand had been set on top to watch over the little town.

The shop windows had been dressed with garlands and cherubs.

The churchyard crib had been scattered with straw. Painted figures gazed at the empty manger where the baby would lie. On the roof, two angels with pink cheeks waited to blow their golden horns.

The children had hung up their empty stockings, full of hope, and left a mince pie and a glass of milk for Father Christmas before tumbling excitedly into bed.

And in the gardens, snowmen and snow babies pulled their scarves a little tighter against the chilly night air as they waited in the moonlight.

Everybody was asleep…everybody except Tilly, who stared up at the night sky, tingling with excitement. She was sure that if she could only stay awake just a little longer, Father Christmas would appear.

Suddenly, a shooting star danced right over the moon. Tilly made a wish and waited, but not a snowflake stirred. She wished again, harder, and listened eagerly for sleigh bells but the snow-hush was deeper than silence.

Then, slowly, a brighter star arose to outshine every other. Almost bursting with hope, Tilly wished a third time. At once, a tiny something flashed across the sky. It twisted to and fro, swaying and swerving, nearer and nearer, with a faint tinkle of bells.

Tilly held her breath — and then she gasped!

Over the rooftops galloped nine reindeer pulling
a sleigh, wildly out of control. And there was Father
Christmas, with one hand over his eyes, holding on for
all he was worth! Tilly watched in astonishment as the
reindeer raced twice around her house and then crash-
landed in the vegetable patch.

Father Christmas tumbled out of the sleigh, rolled
down the garden in a snowball and landed with a bump
at Tilly's back door.

Tilly crept downstairs, slowly turned the door handle and peeped out to see Father Christmas brushing the snowflakes from his whiskers with a chuckle.

"So, it was *your* wish that set my reindeer a-dithering," he said merrily, with a wink. "A wish on the Christmas Star is a mighty magical thing. Well, here I am! But now I shall need your help, Mathilda of midnight miracles, to deliver all these presents!"

Tilly looked at the presents scattered around Father Christmas' crumpled sleigh.

The reindeer, in a cloud of breath, nibbled the holly hedge unhelpfully.

Father Christmas called them all by name — "Dasher, Dancer, Prancer and Vixen, Comet, Cupid, Donner and Blitzen…"

"But where's Rudolf?" asked Tilly.

"Rudolf, chief mischief-maker — come out wherever you are!" called Father Christmas. And with one great leap, Rudolf, who had been hiding behind the chimney, jumped down into the garden.

Father Christmas sent Rudolf to find
more helping hands while he and Tilly
gathered up all the scattered presents.

Tilly found the bright packages easily
in the moonlit snow. But as she hunted in
the shadows of the holly hedge, she thought
she heard the wind whisper her name…

"Tilly, Tilly, open the garden gate…"

Curious, Tilly lifted the rusty latch and pushed
open the gate. There, to her astonishment, were all
the snow babies, in their mufflers and mittens, come to
help Father Christmas!

As they shuffled through the gate, Rudolf returned in
a proud gallop. Behind him, in a sparkle, flew the fairy
from the Christmas tree, the cherubs in their garlands and
the crib angels with their golden horns.

And marching up the path, came a dozen wooden soldiers
leading all the other toys from the market square.

Father Christmas welcomed them all and gave each one a sack of presents. The reindeer let the snow babies climb gently on to their backs. And, with her arms around his neck, Tilly rode Rudolf himself, galloping, galloping up and over the hedge into the starry night sky.

Rudolf landed gently on the rooftops and Tilly
climbed quietly down the chimneys or crept through
open windows. Every child in the little town who had
been good all year had a present from Father Christmas.
Tiptoeing silently, Tilly left each Christmas present in
its place, collected the mince pie that had been left for
Father Christmas and put it into her dressing-gown
pocket.

Anyone who had woken on that
Christmas Eve night and seen
reindeer, snow babies, cherubs,
a Christmas fairy and crib angels
flying in the starlight with their
arms full of presents, would have
thought they were still dreaming.

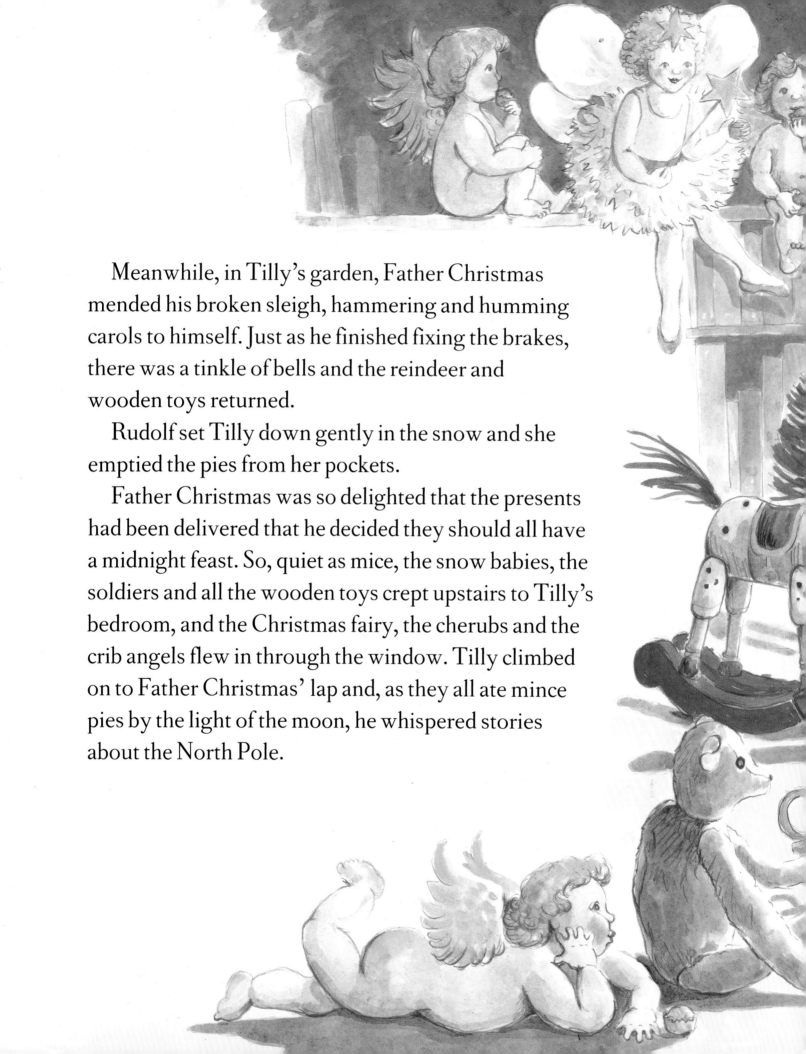

Meanwhile, in Tilly's garden, Father Christmas mended his broken sleigh, hammering and humming carols to himself. Just as he finished fixing the brakes, there was a tinkle of bells and the reindeer and wooden toys returned.

Rudolf set Tilly down gently in the snow and she emptied the pies from her pockets.

Father Christmas was so delighted that the presents had been delivered that he decided they should all have a midnight feast. So, quiet as mice, the snow babies, the soldiers and all the wooden toys crept upstairs to Tilly's bedroom, and the Christmas fairy, the cherubs and the crib angels flew in through the window. Tilly climbed on to Father Christmas' lap and, as they all ate mince pies by the light of the moon, he whispered stories about the North Pole.

Suddenly, the church clock struck midnight. With a yawn, the Christmas fairy said it was time to go and the sleepy snow babies agreed. When everyone had said goodbye, Father Christmas pulled a present with torn wrapping from his pocket.

"What shall we do with this extra one?" he asked,
with a twinkle in his eye.

Tilly looked at the baby doll's face peeping through
the paper and she whispered in Father Christmas' ear.

Father Christmas smiled and, hand in hand, they walked to the church crib. Gently, Tilly lay the baby in the manger under a blanket of straw and, high in the night sky, the Christmas Star blinked brightly. Now Christmas had truly begun!

When they returned to Tilly's garden, they found
Dasher, Dancer, Prancer and Vixen, Comet, Cupid,
Donner and Blitzen and Rudolf snuggled fast asleep.

"Up and away!" called Father Christmas. "Our
night's work is done."
Sleepy Tilly kissed Father Christmas goodnight
and went inside to watch from her window once more.

When the jingling sleigh had finally disappeared beyond the moon, Tilly climbed into bed and there, on her pillow, she found the wand with the golden star — as bright as the one she had wished on that very Christmas night.